CHRISTMAS BRIDE AT ROUGH CREEK

MAIL ORDER BRIDES OF MISSOURI

SUSANNAH CALLOWAY

Tica House
Publishing

Sweet Romance that Delights and Enchants!

PERSONAL WORD FROM THE AUTHOR

Dearest Readers,

Thank you so much for choosing one of my books. I am proud to be a part of the team of writers at Tica House Publishing who work joyfully to bring you stories of hope, faith, courage, and love. Your kind words and loving readership are deeply appreciated.

I would like to personally invite you to sign up for updates and to become part of our **Exclusive Reader Club**—it's completely Free to join! We'd love to welcome you!

Much love,

Susannah Calloway

VISIT HERE to Join our Reader's Club and to Receive Tica House Updates!
https://wesrom.subscribemenow.com/

CONTENTS

CHAPTER 1

The late November rain was turning to sleet as the clock rounded upward toward eleven that evening. Rocking back and forth in time to the tick-tock of the grandfather clock, Dana Wragley glanced up at the old family timepiece and sighed.

"Should be home by eight," Steven had told her that morning when he headed out the door. "Maybe nine at the outside. We've got some shipments coming in, and I'll need to get them in place in the back."

It wasn't the first time he'd stayed at work far longer than he estimated. It wasn't even the first time that week.

"Working too much," she said aloud to the cat, Thomas, who gave her nothing but a slow, heavy blink in response. "When will that boy ever learn?"

He was more than a boy, of course – her son had turned twenty-nine on his last birthday that year. And it wasn't just his age that made him a man. Losing his young wife after only a year of marriage, and the five years as a widower afterward with no one but his mother for company had certainly changed him. Dana watched the fire crackle and twist as she thought fondly, if regretfully, of the innocent, cheerful young man her son had once been—before Anne fell victim to a fever, and the love of his life passed away far too soon…

She had known her own tragedy, losing her husband some years before, but at least that was not entirely unforeseen. Steven's father, Joseph, had been over a decade older than his wife, and sickly besides. His loss was keenly felt, but nothing like the shock of losing Anne. From a mild fever to falling asleep in death, her passing had been completed in only three days, leaving her mourning young husband at a complete loss.

The five years that had gone by since then had wreaked many changes in Steven. He had never been less than conscientious and responsible, but now he spent all his time working the store that his father had left him. It was too much. He was too young to be so totally engulfed in nothing but his work.

Dana reflected that she could not remember the last time she had seen him smile.

With another sigh, she turned to face the window, hoping to see her son's lantern lighting his way home from the store. But there was nothing out there, apart from the patter of the rain and the low moan of the November wind. It would be Christmastime soon – and for Steven Wragley, it was nothing more than a reason to spend even more time at work. His excuse would be that the townsfolk of Rough Creek needed to carry the certainty that the store would be stocked with everything they could possibly need for that season.

It was too bad, Dana thought, that there was no supplier for cheer, for happiness, for love – that was what Steven really needed. Not more time at work, not the approbation of his fellow citizens, not the income that a larger and better stocked store would provide, not even a worried mother, sitting up until midnight waiting for her grown son to come home to the otherwise empty house.

Her son needed love.

But Dana knew in her heart that the chances of Steven allowing himself to love again were very slim indeed. She knew the pain of loss; she knew that there was no recovery unless willpower was involved. And Steven didn't want to change – he didn't want to recover. He took the memory of his wife to bed with him every night, cold on the pillow beside him, tucked all in…

Dana was growing morbid in her old age, she told herself sternly, sitting up straight. It was just the effects of the dark and the cold that were making her feel like this. Why, it was nearly Christmastime. It was time to think of happy things, of family, of warmth and cheer –

And besides, here was her only son, making his way up the inundated path to their front door.

She was sitting with arms folded, her shawl wrapped tightly around her, when he walked into the sitting room. He gave her a tired facsimile of his old smile.

"Ma, I told you, you don't have to wait up for me."

"I was thinking you would be home around eight. Nine at the outset, you said. I was worried."

"Ma, the store's just down the street. What could happen to me between there and home?"

"Bandits," said Dana, aware she sounded a little ridiculous. She rushed to change the subject. "You must be exhausted, poor dear. I've kept the kettle near the hob, let me just set it back on the fire and I'll fix you some tea in no time."

"Thanks, Ma, but I really should just go to bed, as should you. I've got another shipment coming in early tomorrow, I'll be missing breakfast."

She pouted a little – she couldn't help it. Sometimes it felt as though her only family member loved the store more than he did his own mother. He caught sight of her expression and said, placatingly, "I'll try to be home a little earlier, though. Maybe in time for supper. We haven't had supper together in some time."

"That's true," she said. "Steven, don't you think you may be spending too much time at the store?"

"There are shipments coming in, Ma. Someone's got to be there."

"Well, then, why don't you hire another employee?"

"In a little town like Rough Creek? I'm fortunate to have Jack as it is. The only other boys I would trust to run the store on their own are all employed elsewhere, for far more money than I could offer them."

She had run out of valid suggestions and protests. Dana Wragley knew when she was beaten. The only thing left was to drop her head sadly and induce a little guilt. She tried it – the only response was a sigh from her son, and a hand on her shoulder as he went past her.

"I'm beat. I'll see you tomorrow, Ma, if you're up before I leave. Good night."

And then, true to his word, he was gone. Dana rocked back and forth, listening to the crackle of the dying flames and the heavy tread of her son's boots mounting the stairs and going along the hall to his bedroom. She wasn't resentful, she told herself sternly – not of the store, and certainly not of poor Anne, for dying and leaving her son this way. But perhaps she resented the circumstances, for what they were.

Steven was not the same man he had been five years ago.

And without some miracle, perhaps he never would be again.

She closed her eyes. Perhaps that was what was needed – a miracle. Well, this was Christmastime, wasn't it? The perfect time for a miracle to happen. She told herself this in a determinedly cheerful manner, but she didn't fully believe it. Only time would tell.

Dana slept badly that night and awoke to the sound of the door closing downstairs. Steven was gone for the day.

Fighting off a melancholy mood, she arose and went about her chores for the morning, wishing resentfully that something, anything, could come along to distract her from her own sadness. Someone must have been listening to her requests, for Maggie Newton soon came walking up the pathway from the little street, picking her way through the puddles fastidiously.

Dana flung the door open and greeted her friend enthusiastically.

"I'm so pleased to see you. And out in this weather, too."

"Well, it seems as though the rain is holding off – a bit – more or less – so far –"

The friends chuckled as Dana ushered Maggie in. They both knew that good weather was never an option in Missouri in late November.

"Come on along into the kitchen, I was just about to fix myself some more tea."

"Steven's not around this morning?"

"No. Of course, he's down at the store."

"Oh – I thought perhaps since he was there so late last night…Jacob said that the lamps were still lit at eight o'clock, when he was passing by."

"Eight o'clock," repeated Dana. "Goodness, my dear, he didn't come home until after eleven."

"Poor boy, he must be worn out."

Dana poured the tea, shaking her head, and sat down across from her friend at the table.

"I don't know what to do about him, I really don't. Only twenty-nine, and he'll work himself into an early grave if he's not careful."

"Yes," said Maggie sympathetically, but Dana could tell that her friend's mind was not really on the Wragleys' troubles. And, indeed, scant seconds later, she said, "Well, I thought I'd just casually get around to it in the course of things, but I can't contain myself. I have some big news."

"Oh?"

Maggie nodded, excitedly. "Our Edward is going to be married."

Dana nearly dropped her spoon. Edward Newton was a full five years older than Steven and had never so much as gone courting. Privately, Dana had long ago decided that the young man was simply not marriage material, though of course she would never have given his mother her assessment...

"Really? How exciting. And – unexpected, I must say." She wracked her brain for which of the local unmarried women might attach themselves to Edward. She couldn't settle on a likely candidate. "Er...who is the lucky girl?"

"Her name is Kate Spencer. She's twenty-three, brown hair, brown eyes, and worked as a nanny for two years in Boston."

"Kate Spencer? She sounds...lovely," Dana said, secretly rather curious at the odd litany of details that Maggie had spouted off so readily. "I don't believe I've had the pleasure of meeting her – is she from out of town?"

"Oh, I've never met her either," said Maggie, waving a hand airily. "Neither has Edward, come to that. He wrote to a Mail Order Bride agency, and Kate is the match that was arranged."

"Oh, I see." Suddenly, everything made much more sense. "Well, that's very interesting," Dana said. "I never would have thought of such a thing, but it's very resourceful."

"Yes, and, oh, Dana, if you could see this girl's letters. So well-worded, so gentle and feminine. And yet, she's found her own employment, so we know she's not afraid of hard work. And the agency highly recommended her, of course. Edward couldn't be happier, and Jacob and I are rather thrilled, as well – all we ever wanted was for Edward to find a woman who was worthy of him."

"Indeed," said Dana, dropping her gaze to the table. "That's what any loving mother wants for her son, I suppose."

"Kate's train leaves next week, and they'll be married by Christmas Eve and – oh, Dana." Maggie reached out and laid a hand on Dana's, squeezing it in an affectionate way. "Won't Steven consider writing for a Mail Order Bride? Think of it – it would be the perfect way to distract him from work. He could find love again…"

The very thought of it twisted her heart. Regretfully, Dana shook her head.

"He never would consent to it," she said. "He's very independent, and he doesn't think that he needs to change any of his behavior. He's devoted to the memory of Anne."

"Well, after all, they were only married a year…"

But he had intended to be married to her forever. Besides, goodness knows if I suggested such a thing, he'd put his back up, all right. Though it is a lovely thought, and I appreciate you thinking of us, Maggie."

Maggie's face fell a little.

"Well, if you think he really won't agree to it," she said, slowly. "Jacob and I just want your son to be as happy as ours – and for you to be as happy as we are."

"Thank you, Maggie."

The two women sat in silence for a moment, each staring into the depths of their tea.

"Perhaps," suggested Maggie, "what he needs is a surprise Christmas present."

Dana couldn't help but smile. "Now that you mention it," she said, "I happened to be thinking the exact same thing myself…"

CHAPTER 2

Dear Miss Paxton,

We regret to inform you that we are denying your application for employment. Of course, you understand that at this time we have far more applicants than are actually needed, and your experience and skills are not as extensive as others we have received interest from. At this time, we have no need of what you can offer. We wish you all the best.

Hornby and Sons

Naomi folded the paper roughly.

"Wish me all the best," she repeated, huffily. "Well, it's difficult to have the best when no one in the entire world will hire you – lack of experience. How on earth am I supposed to gain experience if no one will hire me because I lack experience?"

She broke off and squeezed her eyes shut tightly, fighting back tears. It took a moment to regain control of her breathing, but she accomplished it.

Taking a deep breath, she put the letter on the pile with the others and stared at them.

"It's been a long six months," she said. "I know you didn't leave me on purpose, Henry – but I wish that you had taken a little worse care of me before you did. Perhaps if you hadn't bent to my every need, I would have learned to fend for myself…"

But there was no point in complaining to Henry. He was far past hearing her.

Henry Paxton had been a good man. Kind, hard-working, respectable and respectful, all the things that were so difficult to find in men these days. From the day he had taken his young wife from her father's home and set up housekeeping in a little apartment in Boston, he had done everything for her, and she had wanted for nothing.

But then tragedy had struck. Henry died suddenly in an accident, and she as his young widow was left with nothing – not even knowledge of their financial standing. It had taken some time to convince the bank that, as his widow, she was entitled to the contents of his bank account. It had taken more time to process the fact that there was scarcely anything there to claim.

Six months – six months, and the savings were gone. Six months of hunting for employment and not finding it. Boston was flush with women who were younger and more skilled than she, and there was no place for her, not even as a nanny or a shopgirl.

The only thing left to do was to move home again...

"And I will not do that," Naomi told Henry's photograph on the wall, fiercely. Flustered by the very thought, she stood and took her coat from the hook, and headed out into the cold November gloom.

Henry's cousin Kate lived only a few blocks away. Kate lived with a flat mate already, a young lady named Lydia Everett, or Naomi would have asked Kate if she was willing to share living quarters. Kate was a year younger than Naomi, had never been married, and was courted by every single man who passed her on the street, whether she was interested in them or not. It was a way to pass the time, she always said.

Naomi adored Kate. She was very smart, spunky, adventurous, beautiful, confident – all the things that Naomi feared she herself was not. And Kate had known Henry, so she understood how Naomi felt. She also knew Naomi's situation as a destitute widow. Simply being in company with someone who understood her feelings and situation was a comfort that Naomi desperately needed just then.

Kate was distracted by something else, however. She let Naomi into the flat, gave her a quick hug, and then hurried back down the little hallway toward her bedroom.

"You're welcome to go into the kitchen and make yourself some tea," she called over her shoulder. "I'll be with you as soon as I can."

Rather than continue to be by herself, or speak with Lydia Everett, Naomi followed Kate to her room. It was a mess. There were clothes spread all around, every which way, and an open valise lying on the bed.

Naomi paused just inside the doorway and stared at it all.

"What on earth are you doing?"

"Packing," said Kate, although the simple fact was obvious.

"But – where are you going?"

"Missouri."

"Missouri? Why? For how long?"

Kate glanced up, hearing the obvious panic in Naomi's voice. She put down the petticoat she was folding and came to her cousin, taking her hands in hers.

"I am not coming back," she said, gently, "because I am going to be married."

Naomi took a few seconds to get over the shock. "Married?"

"Yes." Kate squeezed her hands, then dropped them and went back to her task.

"To whom?"

"A rancher named Edward Newton."

"Kate, I'm quite certain that you don't know any ranchers in Missouri, named Edward Newton or otherwise."

"Yes, that's true," Kate allowed, "but getting married to him will fix that, won't it?" She glanced up again at Naomi's face, and laughed. "Very well, I can see that you're not having nearly as much fun with my being mysterious as I am. The truth is, I signed up with a Mail Order Bride agency two months ago, and they finally found a match I trust in. We've written to each other twice each, since then, and when he asked me to marry him, I said yes. I like him. As much as I can without having met him, that is."

Naomi came further into the room and sank onto the bed, shaking her head in disbelief. "But – every man in Boston wants to marry you, Kate."

"That's as may be," said Kate pertly, trying to pull one of her dresses from underneath Naomi, as her cousin was crushing the fabric. "But I don't want to marry them. I want to marry Edward Newton, in Rough Creek, Missouri, and live on a ranch and herd cattle."

"You want to herd cattle?"

"Well, not me personally," said Kate. "By proxy, I suppose. I'll let my husband handle that part."

Naomi put a hand to her forehead. The tears she had fought back earlier returned, and she was too confused to combat them effectively this time. Kate immediately dropped her garments in a heap on the floor and sank onto the bed next to her.

"What is it, dear?" she murmured.

Naomi shook her head. "It's just – everything, I suppose. I can't seem to find employment, no matter what I do. I've had twenty rejections in just the last month. And I can't keep up the rent on the flat – I don't know what I'll do. I don't want to move back home to my parents'. I'd rather do anything other than that. And I miss Henry – he took such good care of me, I never had to worry – but as it is, I'll be out on the street by Christmas."

The last little bit ended in something of a wail, as she dropped her head into her hands and allowed the tears to overtake her. Kate put an arm around her and listened to her cry for a moment.

Gradually, feeling slightly ashamed of herself, Naomi regained control and lifted her head once more, wiping at her eyes. "I'm sorry, Kate – you've heard me go through this so many times…"

"It's only been six months since Henry passed away," Kate reminded her. "You didn't expect your life together to turn out this way. If you need to cry, you go ahead and cry. Don't apologize to me."

"But I don't want to cry anymore. I want to do something about it."

Kate rubbed at her shoulders. Her expression turned thoughtful. "You said you would rather do anything other than go home to your family?"

"Yes…you know they were against Henry and I getting married, and they've never understood."

"Anything?" Kate pressed. Naomi sniffled and wiped at her eyes.

"Why – what do you mean, Kate?"

But her cousin only smiled, a secretive, joyful smile. "I think you and I should go for a little walk," she said.

CHAPTER 3

"I still can't quite believe that you managed to talk me into this."

Kate laughed. "As I recall, it didn't seem that you took much convincing."

Naomi looked up at the train station and gripped the handle of her bag a bit more tightly. "Well," she said, swallowing hard, "here we are."

Kate's little walk, of course, had led them to the Mail Order Bride agency that she herself had gone to. Along the way, she had explained how it worked to Naomi, and wheedled her to apply for herself. Naomi, reluctant to the last, had finally agreed to do so only on one condition – that the match be somewhere in Missouri, so she and Kate could at least be in the same state.

And then, miracle of miracles – there was a hopeful husband right in Rough Creek, Missouri, the very same place that Kate herself was going to.

"Just remember," Kate told her now, linking an arm through hers and squeezing it against her side, "it's obviously meant to be. Why, you couldn't get any more of a Christmas miracle if you asked Father Christmas for this specifically."

"Perhaps we should wait to meet the men before we decide whether it's a miracle or not," said Naomi.

"You'll never get anywhere with an attitude like that. Why, your man's name is Steven Wragley. He sounds like a fine, strong, upstanding, honorable man to me, with a name like that. And the agent said he owned the general store in Rough Creek. He must be a hard worker, too, and have money to boot."

"Suppose he's a terrible businessman," said Naomi. "Suppose he's lied about his age, and he's actually eighty-seven years old? Suppose he doesn't want to marry me?"

Kate laughed again. "With your positive, sunny outlook on life?" she said. "How could anyone not want to marry you?"

She led her up the three stairs leading into the train car, and Naomi knew that no matter what came next, things would never be the same.

Kate was a welcome and comforting presence on the journey. Naomi's only travel experience had been from her little hometown in Maine to Boston, Massachusetts, six years prior, to marry Henry. Trains were large and loud and unnerving, but Kate embraced the unique experience as an adventure. With her excited reaction to every new piece of landscape that came into view, Naomi couldn't help but start to feel more positive about her prospects – or, at least, this first part of whatever came next. The American countryside was beautiful; so beautiful, in fact, that by the time four days had passed and they were about to puff their way to a stop in

Rough Creek, she was almost regretful that the journey was over.

Or was it apprehension about meeting this Steven Wragley?

She doubted whether Kate had ever felt a moment of apprehension in her life. Her younger cousin fairly bounced toward the train door, anxious to get out and meet her husband to be.

The station was quite small, but it was covered from the apparently relentless drizzle that seemed to pervade Missouri in early December. Clutching her bag, Naomi followed Kate down the stairs. The two women stood together, looking around for someone, anyone, who might be there to collect them.

"Hi there, Miss Kate Spencer. I'd have known you anywhere."

Naomi watched as Kate went eagerly forward to meet the man who was hailing her. He was tall and not unattractive, though Naomi felt he wasn't quite on the same level as Kate. He was a good bit older, too, it looked like—at least a decade. But that wasn't all that unusual, she reflected, and perhaps it was even more normal here in the frontier. Besides, he had a kindly smile, and was greeting Kate with enthusiasm, if also a bit of awkwardness to his manner –

Kate, meanwhile, cast a glance over her shoulder at her waiting cousin, but Naomi waved her on. The last thing she wanted was for Kate to worry about her. Surely this Steven Wragley would appear sooner or later...

"Miss Paxton?"

Naomi looked in the direction of the voice. It belonged to an older woman with steel-gray hair, several inches taller than

Naomi herself, coming toward her with the sort of caution that one might exercise around a wild animal.

"Mrs. Paxton," Naomi corrected her automatically. "My husband passed away only last year."

"Oh, my dear, I am sorry to hear that." The woman's face relaxed into a kindly, motherly expression, and she reached out to Naomi to lay a hand on her shoulder. "I wasn't aware."

Naomi knew she must have a puzzled frown on her face, but she couldn't seem to control it.

"I'm sorry, ma'am – I'm not sure who you are. I believe a young man named Steven Wragley is supposed to collect me. Perhaps you know him, he owns the general store here."

The woman smiled gently. "Yes, yes, he's my son. My name is Mrs. Dana Wragley – you will call me Dana, I hope."

"I – oh." Suddenly, things seemed to clear up, at least a little. Naomi still wasn't certain why Mr. Wragley's mother was collecting her rather than Mr. Wragley himself, but… "I suppose Mr. Wragley is… busy? At the store?"

"Er – yes, as a matter of fact, he is. But that isn't why he's not here. You see…" Dana Wragley wrung her hands together in a worried fashion. Naomi began to get a funny feeling in the pit of her stomach. "The truth is, I have something to confess to you. Steven didn't write to the Mail Order Bride agency. I did."

Naomi blinked. Of all things she had been expecting, this had not even been on the list. "*You* wrote…"

"Yes." Mrs. Wragley nodded.

"I'm afraid I don't understand…"

"He's a widower," the older woman said. "For five years now. His wife died quite suddenly, and – well, he's never been the same since. A broken heart, I guess you could say. But he needs something to bring happiness back into his life – someone." She nodded in the direction of Kate and Edward Newton. "When Maggie Newton told me that Edward had written for a Mail Order Bride and how happy he was, I thought that maybe the same could be true for my Steven."

"I – I don't –" Naomi was having quite a bit of trouble processing this. "He doesn't even know that I was coming?"

"No, I'm afraid not."

"But – I thought I was coming here to be married." She wasn't sure whether she was regretful over this or not. More than anything, she felt confused.

"I believe you will be," said Dana Wragley, holding out a hand to try and calm her. "I believe – I hope and pray – that he'll come around to it. I think it's what he needs, and I hope that he will see that for himself. We will just need to – give him some time. Let him think about it and reach the conclusion on his own. My son is – he's stubborn. Independent. But a good man. He does better if he doesn't think that people are telling him what he should and shouldn't do."

Dana nodded again to Edward Newton, who came toward her now, carrying Kate's bag for her. He nodded in a bashful way to Naomi. Kate, standing close at his side, looked serene as a princess. "I've arranged with Maggie for you to stay with them at their farm. Edward will take you along with – Miss Kate, isn't it? Pleased to meet you. I'm awfully sorry about all the confusion – I'm only trying to do what's best –"

Dana seemed to be trying to convince herself as much as anyone else.

"It was my ma's idea," said Edward, as though this explained everything.

"So you go right along with them, then," said Dana Wragley, not meeting Naomi's eyes. "And I'll – well, we'll see you very soon, I'm sure of it. And everything will work out just fine."

She looked, Naomi thought, as though she felt as unsure about her decision as Naomi herself did. The whole way to Rough Creek, Naomi had second-guessed and doubted herself. And now, to arrive and find that she may not even become a Mail Order Bride after all – well, it was a shock to her to find that she felt rather disappointed.

After all, she'd come all this way.

Kate tucked her arm through Naomi's once more as they stood and watched Mrs. Wragley hurry away.

"That's the thing with life," Kate told her cousin, kindly. "You're just never quite sure how things are going to turn out."

"That's the truth," said Naomi, fervently.

Just once, she thought, she would like for something to turn out like she'd hoped.

CHAPTER 4

As unexpected as everything was, it didn't take long for Naomi to decide that perhaps the way things had turned out was for the best. The short trip to the ranch where Edward Newton lived with his parents, managing his father's cattle, was a bit stressful on its own merits; she had not traveled by horse and cart very often in her lifetime, as she'd grown up in town and then lived in Boston for her entire married life. The racketing and unsteadiness of the cart, which didn't seem to be very well maintained, gave her a headache. Or perhaps it was the exhaustion from the train ride catching up to her – or perhaps it was the confusion of her arrival – but whatever the case, Kate's presence was a blessing and a comfort.

Kate herself seemed to have no trouble whatsoever with discomfort or awkwardness; she chatted lightly to Edward Newton, asking him questions and covering up the pauses when he couldn't seem to think of anything to say. Her attention was obviously both pleasing and embarrassing to him. From Naomi's vantage point on the bench seat at the back of the cart, she could see the tips of his ears turn red every time Kate used his name.

Kate, meanwhile, seemed delighted by him; so there was that worry put to one side, at least. Naomi had a feeling that Kate was going to be just fine, no matter what happened.

Not that she had ever been in doubt.

For her own sake, of course, things were rather more worrisome. How on earth had she ended up in this position? Agreeing to become a Mail Order Bride to a man who had no idea that she even existed – a reluctant participant in a marriage arranged by her betrothed's mother. And there was always the good possibility that the man wouldn't want to marry her anyway – perhaps he wasn't even interested in marriage. Stubborn, independent, always working, a widower for five years running – and those were the words of his own mother. It certainly didn't instill her with any confidence.

Which was, perhaps, the real reason behind her nervousness, headache, and abject gratitude that Kate was there by her side.

The ranch belonging to the Newtons was a few miles out of town, and as they drove, Edward pointed out interesting sights now and then.

"I hope you two will come to love Rough Creek," he said, turning his head to address Naomi as well as Kate.

"Do you love Rough Creek?" Kate asked him.

His ears burned, and he had to think about it for a moment.

"I guess I do," he managed after a bit. "I grew up here. It's all I've ever known. It's not a bad place to be. You'll see."

"I'm sure I will," said Kate, smiling at him. He smiled back, and for a moment Naomi felt a pang of jealousy. She was meant to be speaking to her husband-to-be, too – talking with him, asking questions, exchanging smiles, getting to know him. Instead...

She pushed the thought away from her, along with the resentment. There was no use crying over spilled milk now, she told herself resolutely. What was done was done – all that remained was to see what happened.

The ranch house was a tidy yet generously sized building, and it was obvious from the row of windows along the top that putting up two young visitors was not going to be a problem for the Newtons. As they walked toward the front door together, Naomi whispered, "They must be quite well off."

"Yes," Kate whispered back, "he was very specific in his letters. It may have made quite a difference, otherwise."

There was a motherly-looking woman waiting for them on the front porch, wearing a spotless white apron. She called out to them cheerfully as they approached.

"My mother, Margaret Newton," said Edward.

"Oh, but you two girls will call me Maggie, won't you? I'm so happy to have you here. As soon as Edward told me about you, I knew it was going to be a blessing for all of us." She beamed at Kate, and then turned the beam onto Naomi. "And, of course, we are delighted to have you stay with us. I'm sure that it will only be for a short while, but you are welcome to stay as long as you like."

"Thank you, ma'am," Naomi murmured, reflecting that Edward had claimed that Mrs. Wragley's scheme was his mother's idea. She could well believe it; Maggie Newton seemed like a very persuasive personality.

They were shown into the house and to their rooms. Naomi's initial assessment of plenty of space in the ranch house was quickly proved to be correct. After they had a chance to freshen up and take a few moments to themselves, Maggie called them back down to the kitchen again, where she gave them tea and thick slices of apple pie.

Edward poked his head into the kitchen just long enough to murmur that he would be back for supper, and then darted out again, already blushing. Maggie didn't seem to think there was anything the slightest bit unusual about her only son's behavior and carried on as though nothing had happened.

"Now, I'm so excited that you are finally here. And you too, of course, Naomi. You don't know much about Rough Creek, of course, but the simple fact is that your wedding is going to be the event of the season. And yours too, of course, Naomi," she added, somewhat belatedly. "Now, I've already spoken to the preacher here in town, and he's set aside December Eve day for your wedding – Christmas Eve, and it's a Saturday, which is ideal, for of course you don't want to get married on a Sunday, and Edward works all throughout the week. That will see you happily settled and ready to debut as Mrs. Edward Newton at the New Year's dance in town. As far as announcing it to everyone, the Christmas dance is in just over two weeks' time, and absolutely everyone will be there…"

She went on at length, full of details and plans, and Kate listened politely, interjecting questions or comments here and there. Naomi watched her cousin and knew from the look in her eyes that Maggie Newton's plans didn't matter a whit. When it came to sheer will power, Kate was bound to win out.

"Maggie," Naomi interrupted after a moment, sensing that Kate's politeness was reaching its end, "would you mind telling me a little about Steven Wragley?"

Maggie opened her mouth, closed it again, and hesitated, clearly thrown off track by the question. "About Steven?"

"Yes. I understand that you know Mr. Wragley and his mother quite well."

"Yes, of course. Dana is my oldest and closest friend."

"I must confess, I'm rather confused by her actions. Did she really write to the agency without giving her grown son the chance to express his wishes on the matter?"

She fixed Maggie Newton with a steady gaze and was rewarded with an uncomfortable wriggle of the shoulders from the older woman.

"Well, in a manner of speaking," Maggie said. "The fact is, we know that Steven isn't opposed to marriage – he got married the first time, after all, all of his own volition."

"I see."

"And Dana only wants what's best for her son, of course."

"Of course."

"And besides," Maggie went on, emboldened, "Steven was such a young man when his wife passed on. To devote himself to the dead and gone like that is – well, it's a waste, is what it is."

"So he is still devoted to his wife?"

Maggie realized that she had made an error in her speech, if her goal was to convince Naomi that everything was going to turn out just fine.

"Well, I say devoted," she said. "You'd have to know Steven to really understand. He's – he's a very serious man. He *thinks* about things. If you ask me, he's a little odd – nothing like Edward, though of course, they are friends," she said, shooting a comforting smile at Kate. "He's just – I can't explain him, really. You'll just have to get to know him."

Naomi looked down and pushed the last remaining bite of her pie around her plate with her fork.

"I don't know when I'll get the chance to do that," she said.

Maggie thought about it for a moment, and then brightened up. "Why, I have the perfect idea. We'll invite them over for supper tomorrow to celebrate Edward's engagement."

Kate raised her eyebrows, but before she could speak, Naomi said, "Tomorrow night?"

"Yes, it will be ideal. I've some chickens to prepare, and the table can always seat more visitors. I'll send word through Edward this afternoon."

Kate and Naomi exchanged glances.

"Well," said Kate, "I suppose that would be a cozy way to get to know Edward's friends."

"Tomorrow night," repeated Naomi, more to herself than anyone else. Suddenly, the yawning gap before she could actually meet Steven Wragley had narrowed dramatically, and it was as though there was no time left at all. She'd been anxiously waiting for the end of the train journey, and strangely relieved to have it turn out in such a way –

suddenly, she hadn't escaped after all. A strange mix of excitement and dread began to build in the pit of her stomach.

Kate laid a reassuring hand on her shoulder and squeezed.

"Don't worry," she said. "I'll be right there with you."

CHAPTER 5

When the door opened at five thirty, waking her from her drowse in front of the fire, Dana practically leapt from her chair to run to the hall, patting her hair into place.

"Maggie?" she called as she went. "I wasn't expecting visitors at this hour…"

She stopped and stared. It wasn't Maggie.

"Steven," she said, even more taken aback now. "Well, that explains why Thomas didn't so much as stir – you gave me a fright. I wasn't expecting you back so early today. I'm delighted that you are, of course," she added.

He nodded at her, stomping the last bit of snow from his boots.

"I got word from Edward Newton that we're expected for supper in about an hour. You didn't hear from Maggie?"

"No, not a word. Oh…" She patted again at her hair, and her son favored her with a rare warm smile.

"You look perfectly presentable, Ma. Certainly good enough to visit old friends like the Newtons. I'll hitch up the cart and be ready for you in about ten minutes."

"Did Edward say why we are invited to supper?" she called after him as he threw a warmer scarf around his neck and prepared to head back outside. "It seems rather sudden – or is it just an overflow of festive spirit?"

"Nearly three weeks before Christmas? I hope not. No, he said it's to celebrate his engagement." Steven fixed his mother with a clear, direct gaze. "Apparently, he went through with his fool idea to write for a Mail Order Bride, and she arrived yesterday. Did you know anything about that?"

"I – er – I heard something about it from Maggie," she said. "I didn't realize they were…officially engaged already."

It wasn't entirely a lie. Certainly, she knew that the engagement was inevitable, but Edward Newton had made short work of proposing. Why, the girl had only arrived less than twenty-four hours before. He must have more gumption than she gave him credit for…

Maggie must be over the moon, she thought, a bit enviously.

Steven watched her a moment longer, and then nodded and went outside. Dana exploded into a flurry of preparations. It was true that the Newtons were old friends, and she was long past trying to impress anyone. But still, it wasn't just the Newtons that they would see – it was also Naomi herself, and Dana felt rather anxious that Naomi should think well of her. Especially after the news she had been greeted with when she arrived at the train station the previous day.

Dana couldn't help but feel a little guilty over the poor girl's reaction. Of course, her own actions hadn't been entirely on the up and up. And of course, the girl had the right to be upset. Even as Steven was liable to be, if she didn't handle this tactfully.

She hoped devoutly that Maggie would manage to keep quiet on the subject.

Ten minutes came and went, and she joined Steven outside in the driver's box of the rarely-used delivery cart. They scarcely ever needed a cart to travel, as they lived right there in town, and most of Steven's customers preferred to come into town and do their shopping in person, rather than waiting on the stock boy to deliver their orders. It was only at times like these, when it was getting dark already, and they were heading out to the Newton's, that the tired old mare was hitched up to the cart and asked to drive them the few miles out of town.

It was frigid cold outside. Steven spread a thick wool blanket over Dana's lap and made sure the ends were well tucked in to avoid a draft.

A few minutes into the ride, Dana managed to ask her stoic son, "What do you think of Edward's engagement? Does he seem happy?"

"Happy, sure," said Steven, shaking his head. "Not that it means much – he's hardly known the girl for more than a mere few weeks, and that was all through letters until just yesterday. I said it's a fool scheme, and I meant it."

"What makes you say that, Steven?"

"Why, Ma, just think about it. It's uncertain enough when you know a girl, know where she came from, know her family – but to engage and obligate yourself to someone that you've never met, from goodness knows where? That's foolish, for a certainty. I only hope, for Edward's sake, that she is as good as he insists she is. For all he knows, she could just be after his money."

"Oh, surely not." Dana had been rather distracted by meeting Naomi and had hardly paid much attention to Kate, but she certainly didn't seem like the gold-digging type on first glance.

"I'm not saying it's for sure, I'm just saying it could be, and it would be wise for a man like Edward to be cautious about who he opens up to." He shook his head again. "Edward's not much of a businessman. I tried to give him my perspective, but he's head over heels for the girl already, I can tell. There's no use trying logic on a man in love."

"So you think that it's a poor decision from a business perspective…"

"Well, sure, if you've got a good business, you've got more to attract girls like that, and more to lose. Think about us, Ma. Pa left a good, solid store behind, but over the last few years, I've built it up even more than it used to be. We're the biggest and the most respected general store in the whole county. Folks drive from Allerville and Hawk's Point to buy from us. That makes us more visible to anyone who might decide to try and take advantage – and that makes it even more important that we're cautious."

"Oh," said Dana, deflated. "I hadn't thought of it that way."

"Maybe you should," said her son. "It never hurts to think ahead, Ma." He shook his head once more, muttering to himself. "Poor fool, Edward."

Dana lapsed into an even deeper guilt than before – worse than dragging poor Naomi into this was potentially putting her son in the very position he was so opposed to. How could she have done such a thing? Why, she didn't know anything about Naomi. She was a perfect stranger...

A perfect stranger with a good reputation and a letter of recommendation from the Mail Order Bride agency, she reminded herself. It wasn't as though she had been reckless, inviting the first person she saw in off the street. No, she had done her research carefully, listened to her friend's advice, and above all, she had prayed. She had prayed for guidance, for a miracle...

And she wasn't going to turn her back on that. She had to see it through.

Somehow, things would work out just fine.

The Newton family, along with their two visitors, were waiting for the Wragleys. As soon as Dana reached the veranda, she was pulled into the warm, fire-fed house. Her coat and shawl and muffler were unwrapped from her, a warm mug put into her hands, and she was bustled into the dining room to take a seat before the fire. She found herself sitting just next to Naomi, who smiled at her, a bit guardedly.

On top of all the guilt Dana was already feeling, that guarded smile just about broke her heart. She reached under the table and squeezed Naomi's hand.

"Hello, my dear," she whispered. "I hope that you're settling in well here..."

"Just fine, thank you. Maggie has been very accommodating."

"I can't tell you how sorry I am that things are so very awkward, but – they're going to be just fine, I know it." She broke off as Steven came into the room.

There was a general hubbub and bustle, especially from Maggie, and a cheerful exchange of comments from Kate, Edward, and Edward's two younger sisters. Maggie came forward quickly to introduce Steven to the visitors.

"This here is our Kate," she said, putting an arm around the girl, who smiled at Steven, but quickly allowed herself to be drawn back into conversation with Edward, who was in fine form this evening. "And this here," Maggie said, loudly, to be heard over the chatter, "is Kate's cousin, Naomi Paxton."

Naomi stood from her seat at the table. The room quieted down just long enough for her eyes to meet Steven's with a weight and gravity that seemed to echo.

Steven crossed the room and held out a hand to Naomi, who took it.

"Pleased to meet you," he said.

"Likewise."

"You're staying here with the Newtons?"

She hesitated, but it was so momentary that Dana was sure she was the only one who noticed it.

"For the time being," said Naomi.

Steven cocked his head as though curious, but did not pursue the comment, and Naomi did not elaborate. Jacob Newton, aging patriarch of the Newton family and not a man to suffer the postponement of supper lightly, called for everyone to take their seats.

"It's been a long day," he said, a little irritably, "and some of us want our supper."

Maggie tapped at his arm lightly as she took a seat beside him.

"Oh, you," she said, fondly.

Dana felt yet another surge of envy run through her, this time on her own behalf rather than her son's. She missed being married to her husband. Even though years had gone by, she still felt his absence keenly. Really, she understood how Steven felt; when you lost someone that you loved, there was a strong temptation to curl yourself up around the hole they left behind and growl at anyone who tried to get near.

But that wasn't the path to happiness, not for anyone.

And her son deserved more than that.

She watched him for a moment, and couldn't help but notice that, though he did not speak to her, his eyes returned again and again to the pretty, pale face of Naomi Paxton.

It warmed Dana from within. Such a small show of interest, but it meant so much more coming from Steven…

She had done the right thing, she decided. No matter the risk, no matter the outcome, she had made the right decision.

She'd given Steven a choice in his life and put it right in front of him. She'd helped him as much as a mother could dare.

Now all he had to do was make the decision.

CHAPTER 6

Two weeks had passed since Naomi arrived in Rough Creek – and they had gone by like lightning. The Newtons were sociable in the extreme, and Maggie seemed to be introducing a new friend and citizen of Rough Creek every time Naomi turned around. Naomi was rather grateful that all of these new acquaintances were more interested in Kate than they were in her; Kate handled their scrutiny with her usual grace and calm, and Naomi was perfectly content to stay out of the spotlight.

The only time that this was not the case was when the Wragleys came for supper, as they did twice more after the first occasion.

That first meeting with Steven Wragley had left Naomi rather confused. He was certainly the strong, quiet type, as she had expected from what Maggie and Steven's mother said. But there was something else there – he didn't speak to her much, but every so often she caught him looking at her, and there were unspoken words in his sky-blue gaze.

Then there was the fact that he was far, far more handsome than she had been expecting.

It had truly taken her aback when she first saw him. Dana was tall and slim, so it made sense that her son would be as well, but she had not been expecting him to be quite so tall, quite so rangy, with a head full of ash-blond hair that badly needed a trim. He looked younger than she had thought he would, too – she knew that he was twenty-nine, and that tragedy had marked his features, but still, his eyes were clear and unlined, and his mouth held the shadows of long-ago laughter. He did not smile when they met, and it made her rather sad, as though she had missed out on something.

His tragedy was written all over his face, and she could not help but wonder what he looked like when he was happy – and how long it had been since he was.

Each encounter since then had been much the same. It was Maggie and Dana that did most of the talking – and Kate and Edward, of course, but they had already developed a habit of speaking in a low tone that made it clear they didn't want anyone else to listen in on their conversations – while Edward's sisters and father, Naomi, and Steven all simply listened in. Steven never attempted to corner her, to start a conversation of their own. He never did anything – except look at her.

She had seen him a total of four times, and she was convinced: Steven Wragley wasn't the least bit interested in marriage. Nor was he the least bit interested in her, except as something rather unusual in his small, insular life. It didn't matter what his mother said, or what Maggie professed to believe – he wouldn't reach the conclusion that he should marry again of his own volition, nor would he react well to being told that Naomi had been brought there for just such a purpose. There was no winning in this situation, and Naomi was determined that no one would convince her otherwise. Handsomeness and mysterious sadness aside…

She was reflecting over this conclusion as she helped Maggie and Kate in the kitchen, mixing and baking gingerbread men for the Christmas dance. Kate glanced up at her sharply.

"What is it?"

"Hmm? Oh, nothing. Why?"

"It must be something," said Kate. "You heaved an almighty sigh."

"No, I didn't."

"You did. Didn't she, Maggie?"

"I was certain that I heard a sigh," said Maggie, "but I thought perhaps it was from you, Kate – feeling lovesick and wishing that your wedding day was already here."

Kate laughed. "It certainly wasn't me, but you're right, it did sound rather lovesick." She squinted at Naomi. "Care to tell your old cousin what's going on?"

"I didn't sigh," said Naomi, looking into the bowl she was stirring. "And I'm not lovesick."

She could see Kate and Maggie exchange glances.

"I've been thinking that we should have a little practice session before the dance at the town hall," said Maggie, smiling broadly. "Of course, you have a partner ready-made, Kate, but who should we invite to dance with Naomi?"

"Why, I can't think who might be a good match – someone who she has met before, of course, or she'll be shy…"

"Someone who isn't keen on dancing with other girls anyhow, so he'll be sure to pay plenty of attention to her," suggested Maggie.

"Someone tall and handsome…"

"Why, I do believe that Steven Wragley would be the perfect partner for her."

Kate clasped her floury hands in comic delight. "Why, what a bolt of inspiration has just struck you, Maggie. We should indeed."

"I hear someone at the door." cried Naomi, unable to take their teasing any longer. "I'll just go and see who it is. Carry on, girls."

She fled for the hallway, wiping her hands on her apron. As she neared the front door, however, she felt the beginnings of an irrational fear that Maggie had somehow already summoned Steven, and that he was waiting on just the other side of the door, waiting just to stand and stare silently at her some more…

She gulped past the lump in her throat and flung the door wide open.

Dana Wragley blinked at her in surprise.

"Naomi. That was – quite the welcome."

Naomi heaved a sigh of relief.

"Thank goodness, it's just you. I mean – I'm sorry. Please, come in, Mrs. Wragley."

Dana stepped inside as Naomi held the door open. As she passed, she reached over to pat Naomi on the shoulder.

"I do wish you would call me Dana. I hope that we can be friends...no matter what happens."

Naomi nodded, swallowing hard. "I'm sure that we can, Dana. No matter what happens."

She was not imagining the look of relief in Dana Wragley's eyes.

"Besides," said the older woman, a bit shyly, "I'm certain that things are going to turn out for the best."

Naomi thought of her own conclusions on the matter and debated whether to enlighten Dana – but decided that it was best just to keep her perceptions to herself. Of course, Dana wanted her son to be happy. She would hold onto hope far longer than it was logical.

"Maggie is in the kitchen," she said instead.

Dana nodded gratefully and followed her back into the kitchen. To Naomi's great relief, Maggie had returned to her favorite subject – her son's impending wedding – and the thought of inviting Steven Wragley over for a practice dancing session was forgotten. It was probably only meant as a joke to begin with, Naomi reflected. They couldn't possibly think that Steven would do such a thing – he wouldn't want to lose the time from work, for one thing. He hadn't spoken much in the few times she had been around him, but when he did, his conversation revolved around the general store and his plans for the future. She could understand why his mother was so worried about him. He certainly seemed to be obsessed.

To think of him giving any consideration to any other subject was downright ridiculous. She should put the very idea right out of her head.

There was no chance that Steven Wragley would ever seriously consider marriage to her. Absolutely no chance at all.

CHAPTER 7

Christmastime in Rough Creek was certainly the busiest time of the year. All morning long, Steven dealt with customer after customer, while his stock boy and only employee, Jack, made up parcels and carried items out to waiting carts. It was all this waiting till the last minute that created a problem, Steven thought ruefully. If they would just plan ahead, as he had done, they wouldn't be so worried about getting the things they needed.

Oh, the town was grateful for him, though, and they told him so. Mrs. Curtright thanked him again and again for holding back those two special fruitcakes for her; Mrs. Werner was delighted to find that he had plenty of sugar still in stock, even at this late date. It was scarcely a week until the holiday, and the baking was in full swing. Not to mention the upcoming dance – everybody who was anybody would be there, and every woman who was any woman was bringing a baked good to show off her skills to the rest of the town.

Steven wasn't entirely certain about the Christmas dance, but he supposed he would be forced into going. As the owner of the biggest and most reliable general store in the county, he had a certain presence and a reputation to live up to. He hadn't danced since – well, since his wedding, come to think of it. He'd only been married for a year before poor Anne – it wasn't as though they'd had the chance to attend a lot of parties.

He shook the melancholy thoughts away from his head. What he needed was a little break from work. He didn't do such a thing often, but at times it was necessary – especially at times like these, when he could feel the pressure of his sadness bearing down on him. He had to think about something else.

He untied his apron, calling to Jack. "Watch the store, will you? I'm headed out to get a bite to eat at Hennick's."

Jack nodded and stepped up to the counter. Not for the first time, Steven reflected how grateful he was to have at least one competent helper. There was no way that he could run such a busy and growing concern all on his own.

As he stepped out into the busy street, vaguely observing that snow was beginning to fall, he sought for something, anything, to distract his thoughts from Anne and her loss. Across the street, he caught sight of Edward Newton's broad back, heading into the saloon. Edward was a regular at Hennick's. As rarely as Steven went in there himself, he almost always encountered the lonely heir of the Newton ranch.

Not lonely anymore, he thought. No, their wedding was – well, it was set for Christmas Eve, wasn't it? Only six days from now. Steven liked Edward, though he thought his decision was not the smartest thing a man could do. Still, he'd met Kate a handful of times now, and she seemed like an honest young woman. He would even go so far as to say that he liked her, and that he understood why Edward was attracted to her. Though that talky, over-confident air of hers was rather off-putting, he thought – or maybe it was just intimidating. He much preferred quiet, thoughtful types – like her cousin, Naomi.

There was a thought to distract him from his melancholy…

He plunged through the now two-inch-deep snow and followed Edward into the saloon. His friend was seated at a table in the corner, allowing Ruby, the bar maid, to wish him well on his impending nuptials. She nodded at Steven as he approached and went off to fetch them some plates of lunch.

"Edward."

"Steven."

"How's life treating you?"

Steven could tell from Edward's grin that he was about to say something about his wife-to-be, and sure enough, Edward didn't disappoint.

"Every day, I wake up grateful for what I've got. I know I've only known Kate for a few weeks, but it feels as though I've known her my entire life. I can't imagine living without her."

Looking into his friend's earnest face, Steven decided that his own, much more cynical thoughts on Mail Order Brides were probably best kept to himself. Besides, Edward would be married in a matter of days. Judging by the look on his face, he wasn't about to back out before then. And as happy as he seemed to be, Steven hoped that Kate wouldn't, either.

Maybe she would prove him wrong.

Still, he wasn't all that eager to talk about it, either.

"I'm glad that it's going well," he said, a little stiffly. "I know your ma is thrilled to pieces. She tells my mother every single day." He looked down at the table. "Say, what about Kate's cousin? Naomi?"

"Oh, Naomi?" Edward's grin faltered a little, though Steven was certain that it was simply because his Kate wasn't the center of the conversation anymore. "She's a nice girl. She and Kate get along real well."

"That's, um, nice… is she planning to stay on at your folks' house even after you're married?"

Edward shot Steven a glance that he couldn't quite interpret.

"Well," his friend hedged, "I'm not rightly sure what her plans are."

"Maybe she'll go back to Boston. Maybe she just came out to keep Kate company on the train."

"Maybe."

"Although," Steven admitted with a chuckle, "Kate doesn't seem like the sort of person who seems in dire need of company when she travels."

"No, she does fine whether she's in company or alone, I reckon."

"So – what made Naomi come out here to Rough Creek, then?"

Edward tilted his head at Steven, curiously. He waited a moment while Ruby put their lunch plates in front of them.

"You're pretty interested in Kate's cousin, huh?"

"No, just nosy I suppose," said Steven, cutting up his meat. "I know every story of every person in town. Someone a little different would be a nice diversion."

"Well – I don't know, I guess. She's Kate's only living relative, as far as I know. Not by blood, though – she was married to Kate's cousin, and he died last year sometime."

This fact piqued Steven's interest. He had noted a strange sadness behind Naomi's quiet, level gaze, but hadn't been able to put his finger on what, exactly, it might mean. But learning that she had lost her husband, and so recently, put that sadness in a different light.

"Really…"

"Yeah," said Edward, warming to his theme. "Kate said something about how she didn't want to go home to her family, because they had been against her marriage, and she couldn't find work. I guess there's not much to do in Boston. And then when she heard that Kate was going to come out here and marry me, she decided that she might as well…" He stopped suddenly, and Steven saw the tips of his ears turn bright red. "Well," he said, and coughed. "She decided to come out with her, anyhow."

Steven looked at him curiously, wondering what had thrown him off so badly in the middle of the sentence, but Edward wouldn't meet his gaze. Instead, he looked out the window, and shook his head.

"Snowed a lot in half an hour, didn't it?"

Steven followed his glance. "Yeah. Looks like winter is finally here." That was always the way, in Rough Creek. The weather was rainy and miserable for months before winter properly started, but once the first snow took hold, it didn't let go until March or April. Rough Creek would be snowed in by the end of the day, and other than the main roads through the town, all traffic would occur by snowshoe and sled.

"Going to be a nice white Christmas for the dance – and my wedding." Edward's expression was caught somewhere between joy and smugness, but Steve couldn't rightly blame him.

"All your plans are made?"

"Well, you've met my mother. Could it be any other way?"

The two friends shared a laugh.

"How about the dance, though?" Edward asked him. "We're going to announce our wedding date there – you're coming, ain't you?"

"I don't guess I could avoid it. Everyone expects me. I'll be there."

Edward nodded, satisfaction evident in his face. "Good."

He would, Steven decided for certain. He would definitely be there – he didn't intend to do any dancing, of course, but he would show up.

That was the least he could do, to support his friend and his engagement – even if he did believe it to be foolish.

CHAPTER 8

The town hall in Rough Creek, small as it was, was like nothing Naomi had ever seen before. It was decked out, wall to wall, with pine boughs and garlands of greenery, interspersed with holly and colorful paper flowers that, Maggie told them, were made by all the children of the town. Everywhere, there were oil lamps and covered candles, lighting up the room with a warm, cheerful glow. Along one wall, a series of tables was laid with every type of baked good and covered dish imaginable. There was a small band in the corner, tuning up for an evening of reels and jigs.

Kate reached over to grasp Naomi's hand and squeeze it momentarily.

"It's going to be a night to remember," she whispered.

Naomi had no doubt of it – especially for Kate.

She knew that Kate and Edward were planning to announce their engagement and wedding date that evening. Or, more accurately, Maggie was planning to make the announcement herself. It remained to be seen whether Kate would allow her future mother-in-law to do so, or whether she would take over the job herself. Naomi knew who she had her bets on.

"You enjoy yourself," she whispered back. "I'll – I'll be over there in the corner." She pointed toward a particularly isolated area that seemed well out of the public view.

"Nonsense," said Kate, more loudly this time. "You'll be right there in the thick of things, dancing with every man who asks you – and there will be plenty. This is Missouri, Naomi. Pretty, unattached young women are not commonly seen – and even if a certain storekeeper doesn't get up the gumption to ask you to dance, I'm certain that others will." She towed Naomi along in her wake; Naomi was much smaller than Kate, and the pull was inevitable.

Thankfully for Naomi's nerves, she stopped short of hauling her bodily onto the dance floor, though it may have been simply because she was waylaid by Edward Newton. Edward took possession of his wife-to-be and led her out for the first of the reels. Breathing a sigh of relief and thanks, Naomi scuttled to her chosen corner to hide for at least part of the evening. It was easier to watch the feasting and dancing and merry making from a distance; it was too much to be right in the middle of it.

A young boy brought her a little glass of punch and a plate of spiced sweet bread. She smiled and thanked him, and he grinned a gap-toothed grin and went to serve someone else. The table with all the delectables was not too far from Naomi's vantage point; she observed with pleasure that, even this early in the evening, the gingerbread men that she had worked on with Maggie, Kate, and Dana were nearly gone already.

There really was a special feeling about the town of Rough Creek, she reflected, looking around at all those gathered. It was certainly different from anything she had ever known – and as awkward and odd as things had been with Dana and Steven Wragley, she couldn't help but be glad that she was there.

Where would she be otherwise?

If Henry hadn't died, she would be sitting back in Boston right that minute, in the little flat she had shared with him. But she was surprised to discover, she did not think of that flat as home… somehow, even over the short time that she had been here in Rough Creek, Boston had slipped away from her. She no longer claimed it as her own.

That didn't mean that Rough Creek was her home, either – not yet. But she felt as though she could truly belong here, someday.

She shook her head, feeling tears start behind her eyes. If only things had been a little less complicated…

Who knew how they were going to turn out? The man she had come here to marry wasn't the slightest bit interested in marrying her. And while it was true that there were plenty of other unmarried men in Rough Creek, none of them were rushing up to ask her to dance, despite what Kate had claimed. She was just too plain, too unusual, too new in town – whatever the case, she was alone.

Looking around the bedecked hall, she felt, not the cheerfulness of the holiday season, but an acute sense of loneliness, something deep and welling and overwhelming. She was alone, and reliant on the good will of perfect strangers, who only invited her to stay with them because of her husband's cousin Kate…

As her eyes drifted past the joyous faces, they fell suddenly on the face of Steven Wragley.

Alone, among the people in the crowded hall, he was not smiling. He did not look angry, or sad, as she was – but there was something else in his expression, a vivid watchfulness, something that she had seen before when he looked at her. And he was looking at her now.

Their eyes met across the hall, and their gazes fixed on each other. Though the whirling, dancing couples went to and fro between them, the steadiness of his gaze did not waver.

Naomi felt some strange curling emotion deep within, something she could not name and did not understand.

At last, feeling a blush begin to steal its way up her throat to her cheeks, she broke their locked gazes, looking away. She felt quite light-headed all of a sudden; the hall was too crowded, the music and laughter too loud, the fire burning too warmly. She needed a moment alone.

She stood, all in a rush, and moved toward the door, confident that no one would notice her leave. It was far too crowded for even Kate to realize that she was gone. She would only step outside for a moment; she wouldn't be missed…

Her heart was still beating frantically and erratically, pushed by that unnamed emotion brought on by Steven Wragley's gaze. She stepped outside into the snow, putting a hand to her throat and feeling the double-time jumping of her pulse, hauling in deep gulps of the frigid air.

She closed her eyes, whispering to herself, "Everything is going to be perfectly all right – it's just the heat and the overcrowding that got to you, that's all. When was the last time you were in a room with that many people, after all?"

She sighed deeply and took one more step away from the hall without opening her eyes. That proved to be a mistake; her foot slipped on a slick patch in the snow, and she felt it slide out from underneath her, pitching her backwards as she lost her balance. She gave a small shout, curtailed by her own surprise, and then suddenly she was caught up in a pair of strong arms. She opened her eyes to see the sky-blue gaze of Steven Wragley, his face very close to hers, eyes staring deep into her own.

For what seemed like forever, and yet not nearly long enough, he held her close to him. She felt her heartbeat catch – and then beat faster than ever. His arms were around her all the way, his hand on her back, supporting her. He pulled her up a bit closer, and she thought for a wild moment that he was going to kiss her – and she wasn't sure whether to push him away or pull him closer.

Then he helped her, in a very gentlemanly way, to stand on her own two feet.

Naomi blushed deeply, as much at her own thoughts as at nearly falling on her backside in the snow. Of course, he wasn't going to kiss her. He had no interest in her, and she would do well to remember it.

She cleared her throat.

"Um – thank you, Mr. Wragley."

He nodded politely.

"We've had dinner several times now, and I've saved you from falling into a snowbank," he said. "I guess you could call me Steven if you want to."

She laughed, with the giddy sort of joy that comes from lightheadedness and relief. "Yes – yes, of course. And you will call me Naomi, I hope."

"Since you invite me to, I sure will – Naomi." Another deep nod, and he looked as though he were fighting off a smile. It hovered around the corner of his mouth, and she waited rather anxiously to see if it would win out over his will power.

It took a few seconds, but it did.

The smile emerged as though he couldn't help it, as though he fought it tooth and nail every step of the way – but it was a smile just the same.

He held a hand out to her. "May I accompany you back into the hall? You look like you could use some warming up."

"Oh, yes, I only meant to step out for a breath of fresh air, that's all."

"Got a little more than you bargained for, didn't you?"

She chuckled, and he outright grinned.

"You could probably use a little spin around the dance floor to warm you up, too."

"Oh, I – wasn't intending to dance."

He raised his eyebrows. "Really?" he said. "That's funny. Neither was I."

It happened without her scarcely knowing how. From stepping out of the frigid cold into the warm hall, to being enclosed in the circle of his arms and now swirling in the midst of the good people of Rough Creek – it seemed the work of a moment. She could hardly catch her breath.

All she knew was that this evening hadn't turned out anything like she had been expecting – and much like Kate had predicted, it was one to remember.

CHAPTER 9

Steven Wragley awoke the next morning with the pounding of the reel counting to six in his head, over and over and over...

He stared at himself in the cracked mirror above his wash basin.

"Dancing?" he questioned himself. "Was – was that really you?"

He had to admit that he was mystified by his own behavior of the evening before. He had turned up at the dance fully intending not to dance a single tune. It wasn't as though there was an abundance of available girls to dance with, anyhow – the single men far outnumbered the single girls, as was usually the case in small towns in the Midwest. So choosing not to dance shouldn't be too difficult. No one would even notice.

But then – there was Naomi Paxton, Kate's cousin, the quiet and thoughtful young woman from Boston, about whom he had thought on occasion. And she was sitting in the corner, completely alone, and none of the young bucks in town even so much as approached her.

As the evening had worn on, he'd found himself growing more and more incensed on her behalf. She was very pretty, he had to admit. He didn't understand how the young men of Rough Creek seemed to be missing that. Oh, sure, her cousin Kate was the flashier type of beauty; but Kate was also clearly spoken for and didn't give anyone who wasn't Edward Newton so much as the time of day. So why was the prettiest unattached girl at the dance being completely overlooked by all the men in the room?

He'd realized, partway through the night, that he had taken to glaring heavily at all of the young men every time they walked her way and then seemed to change their minds. Guiltily, he had to acknowledge that his own fixed gaze might have something to do with their apparent reluctance to engage with her. Had he inadvertently given the impression that he himself was interested?

His eyes had strayed to her face, and he had watched the softness of her expression, the clearness of her gaze, for a moment. Suddenly, her eyes had turned toward him, and their gazes had locked.

He didn't know how long they sat like that, staring across the room at each other, but in his heart, it felt like the longest and deepest conversation he'd ever had.

Then she was gone, standing up, practically running for the door. Steven wondered if she had taken ill, suddenly – he felt overtaken by a strong sense of worry, and almost without realizing it, he was on his own feet and following her.

She was standing outside, back to the hall, one hand up to her throat; she wasn't wearing a coat, he noted, which was foolish in the freezing cold. She took a step into the snow and began to slip. He was across the distance and scooping her up in his arms before he even registered what was happening.

And then – well, that had been the real beginning of the problem. That was the real start of waking up with the music still pounding in his head.

He had held her in his arms, and he had pulled her closer.

Her skin was cold, and he knew that she had to get back inside before she took ill. She was a city girl, from Boston – sure, weather could get cold in Boston, but she probably wasn't used to spending much time standing outside in the snow. Her eyes were fixed on his as the lashes fluttered open, and he found himself mesmerized by them. Everything that had held him entranced when they were looking at each other in the hall seemed to be magnified out here, alone together in the snow.

If he hadn't let her go, Steven knew, he would have pulled her even closer still –

And then…

He'd stood up straight and brought her with him, setting her on her feet. She was very slight, at least a foot shorter than he was, and he felt as though he was towering over her like a giant. She looked up at him, and there was a faint smile and a great deal of warmth in her eyes.

Before he knew it – again – he was telling her that she needed to get back inside, and – somehow. – dancing was the surest way to warm her up. And then they were dancing together.

He'd had absolutely no intention of dancing when he had arrived there that evening – how on earth had it happened?

His mind had been awhirl all through the rest of the evening, and he imagined the whispers of the crowd with bitter clarity. Steven Wragley – isn't he still in mourning for his wife? Why, he hasn't paid any attention to a girl in five years.

Though he'd known they must be gossiping about him as it happened, it hadn't mattered much the evening before. Or, at least, not enough to make him change his ways.

Today, though. Today was different.

Today, along with the echoes of the music and the step of feet, he woke with guilt ringing around his head. It was true, he hadn't paid any attention to a woman since his wife had died. He'd loved Anne – he still loved Anne. Five years was a long time to mourn, but mourning was a habit that was hard to break.

How could he think of someone else and still feel that he was being true to Anne's memory?

He closed his eyes for a moment, and the image of Anne's face was in front of him right away, a luminous, long-ago picture of what she had looked like on their wedding day, so young, so carefree, so ready to start their lives together.

Steven sighed deeply and shook himself free of the memory. He was a working man; he couldn't afford to get caught up in the nostalgia and sadness of yesteryear.

What would the townspeople of Rough Creek do without him?

His mother was waiting for him with breakfast, an unusual occurrence as he often left well before she was awake in the morning.

She greeted him with a smile.

"Am I that late this morning?"

"No, not at all – well, maybe just a little. But I got up on purpose to talk to you."

"Oh? What about?"

She handed him a mug of hot black coffee. "What did you think of the announcement last night?"

"The announcement?" He frowned, thoughtfully; it took a moment to come back to him. His head had been so full of Naomi Paxton – and guilt – that he had almost forgotten about the big news of the evening: his friend Edward's engagement to Kate. "Well, we all knew it was coming, didn't we? She was a Mail Order Bride – you have to expect an engagement with a situation like that."

His less than enthusiastic response evidently was not what his mother wanted to hear. Her bright smile subsided a little.

"Well, I suppose that's true," she said. "Still, it's exciting, ain't it?"

"For them, I guess it is."

"Do you feel more certain about Kate, now that you've met her a few times?"

"It wasn't ever really Kate that I felt unsure of," he said. "It's the whole Mail Order Bride scheme." She winced a little at the word, but he plowed on. "There's just so much about it that can go wrong. Any man who lets himself get involved in that is in for a surprise, no matter what happens. If things go wrong, the way in which they go wrong will be unique. And if they go right, it'll be a downright shocker."

Now his mother's enthusiasm was completely dampened. "You sound very cynical, Steven. I didn't raise you to be that way."

"I know," he said, relenting somewhat at the expression on her face. He stood, draining the last of his coffee, and planted a kiss on his mother's head, a rare show of affection. "I'm sorry. I don't mean to be like this – it's just how things have turned out, I guess."

"Steven," she called after him as he headed for the door to start his workday.

"Yes, Ma?"

She smiled at him, though it looked a bit tremulous, as though she were fighting back tears or some strong emotion.

"I was glad to see you dance," she said, simply. She left it at that, and Steven decided it would be best if he did, too. She wasn't pushing for him to court Naomi. She wasn't pushing for him to get engaged like his friend had done. And most importantly, he thought, she wasn't asking him to write for a Mail Order Bride.

His ma was smarter than that, he thought.

All through the rest of the day, he caught himself humming the tunes that he and Naomi had danced to; and each time, upon realizing what he was doing, he thought of Anne.

It was the longest day he'd had in a very, very long time.

CHAPTER 10

The wedding dress was as white as the snow that blanketed Rough Creek. It was made of a thick material that Naomi could not name and had been altered to fit Kate like a glove.

"Altered rather dramatically, as you might guess," Kate told her, fluffing the folds of the skirts that fell around her like an old-fashioned ball gown. "It belonged to Maggie, you know."

Naomi stifled a giggle.

"Did they save the extra pieces?" she said. "You never know, I might need a wedding dress of my own someday, and I reckon there might be enough there to cover the pattern."

Kate giggled outright, and pinched Naomi on the arm.

"Now, that's my mother-in-law you're talking about. If there's teasing to be done, I should be the one to do it." She turned to face herself in the full-length mirror at one end of the room. It had been specially borrowed for the occasion, as very few households had such a thing in Rough Creek. Kate smoothed the folds of the dress down around her and adjusted the shoulders and cuffs at the wrists of the long sleeves. "It is rather amazing that it's in such good shape, and still so perfectly white. It must be thirty years old."

"Why, it's older than both of us."

Kate smiled at her reflection in a pleased way.

"And it looks good for its age," she remarked.

Naomi sighed happily. "You look beautiful, Kate," she told her cousin.

Kate glanced out the window at the falling snow outside. It was Christmas Eve, and the weather knew it. The light snows of the last few days had been nothing compared to this.

"It's a good thing that we're getting married soon," she said. "or we wouldn't be able to get through the streets to the church. And I'm so pleased that Dana was able to lend us their house to hold the reception in – they're still cleaning up the hall after the Christmas dance, you know."

"I know. I wanted to go and help, but Dana needed a hand with getting the house ready."

Kate glanced slyly over at her friend, who was picking at the bouquet of greenery that she would hold as she walked down the aisle of the church.

"And how are things going over at the Wragley household? You've spent quite a lot of time with Dana since the dance, haven't you?"

"Oh, a fair amount. She really is a very sweet person, though it was all so awkward when I first came to Rough Creek. But

I like her, and I know that she means well with everything she does."

"She likes you, too. She hasn't given up on you and Steven – and neither have I, for that matter."

Before Naomi knew it, she was blushing. "Oh, I think that ship has sailed," she said. "He doesn't want to be married – it's obvious by everything he does."

"Oh, is it? It's obvious by the fact that he dances with you for hours? It's obvious by the fact that every time you two are together, his eyes are fixed on you? It's obvious by the fact that apparently he hasn't paid a lick of attention to a girl since his poor wife died, and suddenly you're here and everything's different?"

Naomi shook her head, knowing that arguing with Kate was futile. "I don't think it's like that," she finally said. "I mean, yes, of course, he did dance with me – and it took me by surprise as much as anyone else, I promise you."

"I've never seen a woman look so happy as Dana did when he led you out onto the floor."

"But that's been a few days now, and even though I've been at Dana's, he hasn't so much as spoken to me."

Kate whirled on her. "So you have been spending more time with Dana Wragley to test out whether he has any feelings for you." she crowed triumphantly. "I knew it – even though you've been trying to avoid the subject these last few days."

Naomi bit her lip, trying to compose her thoughts. "It's true, I wondered," she said. "I had been so certain that he wasn't interested in me, but then the night of the dance – well, any girl would wonder. There's no harm in that. But the last few days have just proven me to be correct, Kate. No matter what you say, no matter what his mother does – no matter what I do – Steven is still true to the memory of his wife. No one is going to change that except Steven himself."

Kate shook her head in dismay.

"He seems like such a smart man," she said. "You would think that he'd realize he can't be happy living in the past. Look at you, Naomi – you were true to my poor cousin Henry, and you loved him dearly while he was alive. But missing him won't bring him back, and neither will barricading your heart away from any other chance at love. You're braver than Steven Wragley."

Naomi smiled sadly. "And a great deal of good it's done me," she said softly.

She didn't fault Steven Wragley for not wanting to marry her, she really didn't. He owed her nothing; he hadn't made any promises, and he hadn't even been the one to write to the agency for a bride. None of this was his fault.

But she couldn't help being a bit saddened by it all. Those few moments spent in his arms, that all too brief time… it had made her believe that she could be happy again. And that she could be happy with him.

But that wasn't the case. And there was no use crying over it, she told herself sternly. She would just have to find some other way to be happy, that was all. After all, she had the rest of her life to look forward to.

Kate took her arm. "Naomi? Are you all right?"

Naomi dashed the tears out of her eyes and turned a too-bright smile on her cousin.

"I'm just so happy for you," she said. "I can't help but be emotional – you're about to be married."

She could tell that Kate didn't fully believe her explanation, but there was someone calling for them from downstairs, and there was no more time for arguing. It was time to go to the church.

Two closed carriages took the Newton family, along with Kate and Naomi, from the ranch to the church in Rough Creek. The church itself had been decorated on the inside with wreaths, garlands, and candles; on the outside, the dim light of the noon sun shone through the snow clouds and illuminated the streets. There was already a thick blanket of snow on the church roof, and the wedding-goers had to pick their way through the drifts as well as they could. It was indeed a blessing that the Wragleys had offered their home for the wedding reception, Naomi thought; it was very close, right here in town, whereas the road to the Newton ranch was difficult to travel. If it weren't for Dana and Steven and their generosity, there would be no reception at all.

And this was a day that should be celebrated.

The wedding itself was very simple; Naomi stood and watched as Kate and Edward said their vows with tears of joy shining in their eyes.

She had to fight back a few tears herself.

And then, suddenly, it was over. Edward took his wife by the hand and turned to face the assembled guests, who cheered so loudly that the sound rebounded off the rafters and overflowed out the open double doors into the frosty street outside. Kate was married – and the Mail Order Bride agency back in Boston had another success story to tell.

It was too bad, Naomi thought briefly, that her own story would end quite differently.

She shook the thought out of her head. This was a day to focus on the happiness of her friend, not to dwell on her own sadness. After all, tomorrow was Christmas day. Who knew what tomorrow would bring?

CHAPTER 11

Steven had to admit, it was a beautiful ceremony; and, he was certain that the key to its beauty lay in its simplicity. No one was trying too hard. Kate was wearing her mother-in-law's wedding dress. They were going back to Steven's house for the reception. It was snowing.

Simple. Beautiful. Perfect.

He couldn't help but think of what his own wedding had been like, some six years before. It had occurred during the summertime, of course, so most elements had been different. And Anne had been a much more complex woman, with more plans and ideas than she knew what to do with. It had been a big party. Dancing, cake.

And then, a year later, the wedding was a memory – and so was poor Anne.

This wasn't the time to dwell on his own sadness, he told himself firmly. This was the time to focus on the happiness of his friend. Edward had been married, and successfully, too.

Playing the host was not Steven's strong suit. He was much more comfortable helping his customers find what they were looking for or writing down orders for the future. But here he was, with half the town jam-packed in his own house, wandering around trying to do what he could to make things go as easy as possible.

Not that anyone was being difficult. There was punch and cake everywhere he looked; everyone seemed to have entered into the spirit of things. And no one even seemed to be all that concerned about the snow that continued to fall thickly. Near three feet and counting, he estimated – but here in the house, with the fire and all the bodies in close company, no one was the least bit worried about the cold.

They'd figure out getting home later, he knew, although it was going to be difficult. He wasn't entirely sure how the Newtons themselves were going to get back to their ranch that night. The roads must be piled high by now…

He meandered back through the house, exchanging pleasantries with friends and acquaintances and customers, and found himself thinking about Naomi.

Thinking about Naomi had become his new pastime. Indeed, it seemed that any moment in which his mind was not actively occupied with something else, she popped into it and took over. It wasn't that she was the bossy type, of course – she wasn't demanding in his thoughts. It was just that she was pervasive, and persuasive – and he was weaker than he thought.

If this had been a summer reception, he knew, they would be packed into the town hall again, or gathered into a field outside. And there would be dancing – and he would dance with Naomi, he was certain of it. He had absolutely no confidence in his ability to turn away, should the opportunity arise.

Just as well that there would be no dancing tonight…

He made his way toward the kitchen, deciding that he should at least find out whether his mother needed any help.

Getting there was a bit of a chore – there was a throng of people just outside, all talking animatedly. He began to excuse his way through but caught bits and pieces of conversation coming from within the hot kitchen.

"A beautiful ceremony, wasn't it? You'll want to watch that bread, I'm afraid it will burn." It was his mother talking.

A pause, and then a voice that he readily identified as belonging to Naomi Paxton.

"It was gorgeous," she said. "And so simple – I think that's what made it so beautiful, really. They didn't need elaborate flower arrangements or organ music – they only needed each other, standing together, holding hands."

"Yes," said Dana Wragley, and he could tell she must be smiling. "Such a sweet ending to their story."

"And the beginning to a new chapter."

"I hope that things will turn out much the same for you, my dear."

Steven stiffened, wondering what his mother could be referring to. Naomi had been over to the house several times over the last few days – had she confided in Naomi about an impending courtship? Something that he hadn't heard about yet? Something that perhaps had started at the dance – he'd thought that none of the men had approached her, but he was the first to admit that he could have been wrong. She was such a pretty girl, it seemed natural to hear that she was expecting an engagement.

So why was he so upset over the very notion?

A moment went by, and then Naomi said, so quietly that he could barely hear her, "I don't believe that I have the same storybook ending in my future that Kate did, Dana – at least, not like you hope."

"You may think that, my dear, but I think differently."

"He hasn't so much as spoken to me…"

"Ah, but I've seen how he looks at you. And I've seen a difference in how he behaves. He doesn't rush off to work like he used to every morning, and he hasn't come home late a single time since he first met you, I don't believe. Why, he's even been smiling more. There's a change in Steven – a good change."

Steven caught his breath. They were talking about him.

"I haven't noticed," said Naomi. "Though I can't imagine him much different – he's already quite perfect, of course."

"I can't argue with that because I am his mother – but he is certainly lacking something, and that is a wife. I expect that will be remedied sooner or later – for your sake, I hope for the sooner, but we can't rush these things, after all. He's only known you for a few weeks, and I can already see that his life has changed for the better." Dana chuckled. "Yes, I know it was awkward for you when you arrived, my dear, but I do believe that I did the right thing in writing for a Mail Order Bride for my Steven. And I'm so pleased that you are the one that the agency sent. You are the Christmas gift that we needed."

Steven swallowed hard; there was a lump in his throat that was growing rapidly. He couldn't move. Had he just heard correctly? Surely, he was mistaken. Surely, his own mother hadn't plotted behind his back. It pained him, and he felt the betrayal to his toes. From his own mother – *and from Naomi.*

He glanced around. He needed to get out of there, but there was nowhere to go. And the sooner he confronted his mother, the better.

He finally made it to the doorway of the kitchen and stepped inside. He could tell from his mother's face that she realized he'd heard her words –it must have shown in his expression.

He swallowed again, trying to clear his throat so his voice would come out as usual. But it sounded rather stern and harsh, even to his own ears.

"Mrs. Paxton," he said, "would you give me a few moments alone with my mother?"

Naomi nodded wordlessly and rushed out of the kitchen. Steven folded his arms and fixed his mother with a stern glare.

"I hate to ask you to explain…"

She put her hands up. They were shaking slightly. "I'm ready to apologize for doing this without your knowledge," she said, quietly and rapidly. "But I won't apologize for doing what I thought was right. It's been – difficult, of course. But you have to admit that what I said wasn't wrong. You're happier, now that Naomi is around. You're better…"

He shook his head and held up his hand to stop her. "Ma, you had no right to meddle in my life this way, no matter that you thought it was the right thing to do. I'm a grown man—"

"You're letting your life slip away," she cried. "Steven, you are my only son, my only child, I can't stand to watch you spend the rest of your life alone and unhappy—"

"Like *you?*" he said frankly. "Pa has been gone for a while now. I don't see you out there looking for some new love to make your life complete."

Her gaze faltered and fell away from his. "Th-that's different…your father and I had so many happy years…"

"And is it Anne's fault that she and I only had one?" He shook his head. "It's just the way things turned out, Ma. And it still makes me hurt to think about it, just like it still makes you hurt to think about losing Pa. Love isn't less important because it doesn't last as long."

Her head was lowered, and he had a sudden guilty suspicion that she was weeping. He went to her and tentatively put his arms around her. "I know you meant well," he said, "but it wasn't your place. You can't arrange love as though it's a bouquet of flowers."

She looked up at him through teary eyes. "But you care for Naomi, don't you?"

Steven swallowed. "Yes," he said slowly, "I reckon I care for her. She's a nice girl, Ma. She's good company. That doesn't mean you should have written for a bride on my behalf."

Dana sniffed and nodded, putting her arms around her son. They held each other for a moment.

"I-I'm sorry," she said. "I only want what's best for you."

"I know, Ma."

"And for you not to spend all your time working."

"I know, Ma, I'll try to be home more."

"And for you to be happy."

He heaved a sigh. "I'm working on that," he said softly.

They stood for another long moment, and then Dana put her arms down and stepped away from her son, wiping her eyes.

"You'd better go after poor Naomi," she said. "It's my fault, of course, not hers. She didn't know. But I reckon she thinks you're angry at both of us."

"Sure, sure, I'll go find her. I'll bring her in, and we'll all make up and start over." He gave her a reassuring nod and went out into the sitting room. The room was still packed with guests, none of whom seemed the least bit inclined to leave, but Naomi was nowhere to be seen. Steven felt the beginnings of worry start to stir and hunted through the rest of the downstairs rooms to no avail.

Coming back into the sitting room, he reached out and caught hold of Maggie Newton's sleeve.

"Maggie, have you seen Naomi?"

"Why, she went past me and ran for the front door, a little bit ago. She seemed as though she was running from something – I thought I heard raised voices – is everything all right?" She blinked innocently at him, and Steven narrowed his eyes back at her. He had a sudden suspicion that his mother had not concocted this scheme all on her own.

But this wasn't the time to press the issue. Naomi was outside, and if the Christmas dance was anything to go by, she likely didn't even take her coat. He would have to go and fetch her before she caught her death.

He stepped out onto the porch, buttoning his own coat, ready to call to her.

On every side of the porch, in every direction, the snow had fallen, pristine and white. And Naomi was nowhere to be seen.

CHAPTER 12

"You go north, I'll go south, and you two can head eastward toward the meadows – does anyone have any questions?"

It had taken only a handful of minutes to turn the wedding guests into a search party. But even five minutes was a long time in the cold and the snow, and the nightfall came early on winter days like this. Already, the light was threatening to fade, though it wasn't even four in the afternoon. Steven squinted anxiously at the sky as though he could turn back time.

"If we could just tell where she might have gone," he said, helplessly. "If we could see some tracks…"

"Snow's falling too fast for that," said Jacob Newton sternly. "She's a bright girl, hopefully she hasn't gone too far."

"But where would she have gone, anyhow?" asked Kate, wringing her hands. "It's Christmas Eve, and everyone she knows is here…"

"The train station," said Dana. "Would she have gone to buy a ticket?"

"Why would she buy a ticket?" cried Kate. "Why'd she leave anyway?"

Dana met Steven's eyes, then looked away. "She may have been under a mistaken notion…"

"It was a misunderstanding," said Steven. "That's all. She might think I'm upset with her – but I'm not." Which wasn't exactly true. He had been upset with her, but he wasn't now. He put his arm around his mother's shoulders. "Train station is to the north. Jacob can check that out as he goes."

As the respective search parties split up to go their ways, Dana turned to Steven beseechingly. "Please find her – it's my fault that she's here."

"It's my fault that she ran away," he told her. "I shouldn't have been so angry."

"I wish we knew where she was…"

An idea popped into Steven's head. "Do you think she might have headed back to the Newton ranch?" he said slowly. "It's a long way, but she probably doesn't even understand how dangerous it would be to go back on foot in the snow."

Dana nodded slowly. "No one was going that way out of town, were they?"

"No, they're all looking closer to home."

"Will you go and check, Steven? I'll never forgive myself if…" Her voice faded.

He reached over her head and took her heavy wool coat from where it hung on the wall. "I'd better take this with me, just in case."

He plunged out into the snow without another thought, knowing that it was only a matter of time before Naomi would freeze to death. She wasn't used to the winter here in the wilds of Missouri. She didn't know what this sort of snow was like. But if she thought he was angry at her, she would have run away – and there was nowhere else in Rough Creek that she knew as any sort of home.

He wished the snow was manageable enough to take a horse instead of going on foot. But there was nothing for it. He pushed on, mostly able to stay on top of the drifts, but falling through now and then. The cloth of his trousers was quickly soaked through above his tall boots, and he shuddered to think how cold and wet Naomi must be after more than half an hour out there in the snow. If only he had kept his anger in check –

He felt the old familiar guilt, but it was for a different purpose, this time. He had caused this, though not intentionally. He had made her run away – from him.

When he found her, he promised himself, he would make it up to her. No matter how long it took, he would make it up to her.

The realization came to him with a suddenness that felt like a physical blow. He had told his mother that he cared for Naomi, and it was true. But now he knew the truth of it. He was beginning to love her.

His own words echoed in his mind – you can't arrange love like a bouquet of flowers. Well, that was exactly what his mother had tried to do, and somehow, that was exactly how it had turned out. He loved Naomi – not the way he still loved Anne, after all this time, but with a love that was just beginning.

He had to find her.

He was nearly halfway to the Newton ranch, and the snow was falling thicker and faster than ever. The guilt and the worry spurred him on, and finally his efforts were rewarded. Ahead of him, half covered by the snow, he saw a dark figure lying in a drift.

"Naomi!"

He plunged onward and was at her side in mere moments. Her eyes were closed, and she was terribly still. For a moment it seemed that his heart stopped, and he fell to his knees beside her, gathering her up in his arms.

"Please," he whispered to her still figure. "I can't – I can't lose someone else that I love."

He felt the rise and fall of her breathing, and was up on his feet again, carrying her, heading as quickly as he could for home through the gathering dusk.

The rest of the evening was a blur, filled with faces and talk and someone giving him a mug of hot tea, and someone else reassuring him that she was going to be just fine. Everything, they said, was going to be just fine.

He didn't dare believe them – and so he asked again and again. He received the same answer every time. Finally, Doc Shields, who had fortunately been in attendance at the wedding reception, said, irritably, "I've said she's going to make it, and I meant it every time I said it. It was a close call, but you got her back in time. Now sit down before you fall down, young man."

He wasn't sure if he sat down or fell down, but either way, he ended up in a chair.

As he finally nodded off later, he had dark and worrying dreams, though he knew all through it somehow that he was safe and warm and resting at home. In the middle of the dreams, when things seemed darkest, he opened his eyes and saw Naomi watching him.

She smiled.

Hardly daring to believe it, he smiled back.

"Hello," she whispered.

"Hello." He looked around himself. He was in an armchair in his mother's room, and she was swathed in mountains of blankets in his mother's bed. They were scarcely two feet away from each other. If he wanted to reach out and touch her, he could.

With a trembling hand, he reached out.

Her hand met his halfway, and they clasped hands across the distance.

"You saved me," she said.

"It was my fault that you ran away. I wasn't angry with you – not really. I-I was caught by surprise…"

"I'm sorry I didn't tell you the truth right away," she whispered. "I should have."

He shook his head. "It doesn't matter now. All that matters is that you're here – you're safe."

"I heard you say something when you rescued me," she said.

"Yes?"

"You said, you couldn't lose another person that you loved."

Steven bit his lip. "Are you certain that was me?" he said, his voice now light. "You were frozen – dreaming –"

She laughed and squeezed his hand. He squeezed back, suddenly happier than he had been in a long, long time.

"You're right," he said softly. "I did say that. And I meant it. And do you know what else, Naomi Paxton? It's Christmas Day."

Her hand was warm in his. "What happens now?" she asked him.

Steven Wragley couldn't help but smile. "I have a pretty good idea," he said, "and I have a knowing that it's all going to turn out just fine."

He laughed again as he said the words—knowing this time they were true. Everything *was* going to turn out just fine, as long as Naomi was by his side.

The End

Thank you for reading *Christmas Bride at Rough Creek!* **Are you wondering what to read next?** Why not read *Christmas with Michael?* **Here's a peek for you:**

The winter was long in coming to Shallow Gorge that year. The cold weather that traditionally started around October, or even earlier in Colorado, seemed to be holding off, almost as though summer itself was reluctant to pass by. But at the end of November, finally, the first hard snow fell, and Ginny Jones felt that she could breathe a little deeper with the heat of the summer in the past.

She had often heard that a person doesn't get over a loss — they only get through it. Each day that went by was a little further from Edwina's passing. Ginny found herself counting the days, while still feeling guilty over wanting so badly to forget.

Her parents did their best to help her. Ginny's father, a stoic man who was only rarely given to displays of emotion, put his arm around her now and then, a comforting presence though he didn't speak much about what had happened. Ginny's mother, Hannah, sat with her through her long nights without sleep, telling her over and again that she mustn't blame herself.

And still, it seemed as though Edwina was always there with them, a talkative, imaginative eight-year-old, a whole ten years younger than Ginny herself, running after her older sisters and tugging at their skirts for attention.

Sometimes, Ginny wondered if she wasn't haunted.

The snow seemed to help. It blanketed the little farm with a clean whiteness, softening the everyday sounds of the world around it. There was always plenty to do, of course, and that helped, too — when she wasn't helping her mother in the kitchen, Ginny was milking cows, feeding animals, carrying water, or turning her hand to the homemade goods that the Jones girls always crafted each year, for sale as presents during the holiday season. Ginny was as fine a whittler as any boy her age, and deft with a knife. She made toys, and her younger sisters, Jill and Molly, painted them. The general store in Shallow Gorge, run by an enterprising young man named Henry Henderson, always stocked as much as they could give him, and usually sold out besides.

Yes, the work never stopped at the little Jones farm, no matter what time of year it was — and Ginny was grateful for it.

On the second of December, shortly after breakfast, they heard the sound of horse hooves, crunching through the frozen snow. Ginny looked up from the dishes she was scrubbing, catching her mother's wide-eyed gaze.

Visit HERE To Read More!
http://ticahousepublishing.com/mail-order-brides.html

ABOUT THE AUTHOR

Susannah has always been intrigued with the Western movement - prairie days, mail-order brides, the gold rush, frontier life! As a writer, she's excited to combine her love of story with her love of all that is Western. Presently, Susannah lives in Wyoming with her hubby and their three amazing children.

www.ticahousepublishing.com
contact@ticahousepublishing.com

www.ingramcontent.com/pod-product-compliance
Lightning Source LLC
Chambersburg PA
CBHW061249140726

47998CB00006B/2157